FLEISCHMAN

A CARNIVAL OF ANIMALS

Pictures by
Marylin Hafner

GREENWILLOW BOOKS • *An Imprint of HarperCollinsPublishers*

Watercolors, colored pencils, and
pen and ink were used for the full-color art.
The text type is Trump Mediaeval.

A Carnival of Animals
Text copyright © 2000 by Sid Fleischman, Inc.
Illustrations copyright © 2000 by Marylin Hafner
Printed in Singapore by Tien Wah Press. For information address
HarperCollins Children's Books, a division of HarperCollins Publishers,
1350 Avenue of the Americas, New York, NY 10019.
www.harperchildrens.com

Library of Congress Cataloging-in-Publication Data
Fleischman, Sid, (date)
A carnival of animals / by Sid Fleischman ; pictures by Marylin Hafner.
p.   cm.
"Greenwillow Books."
Summary: Tall tales about the fantastic adventures of
some of the animals that live around Barefoot Mountain.
ISBN 0-688-16948-1 (trade). ISBN 0-688-16949-X (lib. bdg.)
[l. Tall tales.] I. Hafner, Marylin, ill. II. Title
PZ7.F5992 Car 2000   [Fic]—dc21   99-053524

1 2 3 4 5 6 7 8 9 10   First Edition

For Dorothy Albee — S. F.

For Katherine, Samuel,
Sarah, and Zoë — M. H.

CONTENTS

The
Windblown
Child

A no-account little tornado came twirling like a ballerina across the countryside. It meant to do no great mischief. It went this way and that, jiggety joggedy, as if to show off its swirling brown veils.

When the tornado bumped into a forest of cottonwoods, the trees did have to hang on to their leaves with all their might. But soon the twister had whisked itself away east of Barefoot Mountain, and the animals climbed out of their burrows and shelters.

It was a raccoon who first spotted the strange little animal, all pink skin and bones, lying in a heap against a hollow log.

"Where do you suppose *that* came from?" muttered the raccoon.

"The tornado must have picked it up somewhere and dropped it here," said Clarence, a pack rat, crawling out of the hollow log.

"What is it, do you suppose?" asked the raccoon.

"A skinned something or other," said Clarence. "The tornado must have plucked out all its fur."

"I wonder if it's alive," said the raccoon.

The show-off squirrel, who liked to be in the center of things, put his ear close to the creature's face and listened.

"That bag of bones is breathing," he said. "It could be a newborn pig."

"It don't have a snout," said Clarence, who had an eye for detail.

Said a woodpecker, "Look, it's beginning to shiver."

"You'd shiver, too, without your feathers," said the

raccoon. "Clarence, you're always dragging back stuff to hoard away. Give us some rags to warm this windblown child."

So Clarence dug into his treasures and came up with a couple of potato sacks, and soon the strange visitor was bundled up.

The forest animals began calling the creature the Windblown Child until she might come to her senses and tell them what in tarnation she was. A goat? A plucked fox? A dangerous bobcat, even?

The Windblown Child discovered that while swirling inside the tornado her wits had got scrambled. What was she doing here? She couldn't remember who she was or what she was.

Soon the Windblown Child sprouted speckled wool that grew lickety-split down to the ground. You could barely see her legs.

Clarence noticed that on her left side those legs were as

long as broomsticks. They appeared to be growing faster than the two on her right. Those were as short as the legs on a footstool. Clarence wondered if the tornado had done that to the stranger. Maybe the two slow legs would catch up.

But they didn't, and the Windblown Child couldn't walk on such uneven legs. She'd tip over, *kerplunk.*

Kerplunk! Kerplunk! It was while the Windblown Child was picking herself up that Thump Oswald swooped down from the sky and grabbed a perch on a cottonwood limb. Thump was a know-it-all red-tailed hawk.

"Hey, runt," said the hawk to Clarence. "You can't teach that critter to navigate the flatlands. Its legs ain't built for it. You know what you got there?"

Clarence was on guard, for he knew Thump Oswald to be as slick as bear grease. "No business of yours."

"What'll you give me to tell you what it genuinely is?"

"Not a thing, sir."

"I'll be neighborly and tell you anyhow," said the red-tailed hawk. "I seen a few of those varmints over in Barefoot Mountain. It's half sheep and half long-haired mountain goat."

"You don't say," murmured Clarence.

"And the other half spotted leopard. You can see the spots for yourself. I wouldn't get too close, Clarence."

"Flapdoodle, sir."

"That dangerous varmint is a Sidehill Clinger."

Clarence had never heard of such an animal. "A Sidehill Clinger, you say. I'll try to remember."

The Windblown Child looked up as if something had stirred her memory.

"You know how confounded steep-sided that mountain is, don't you?" continued the hawk. "I've seen mountain goats that needed ropes and stuff to climb to the top. But not Sidehill Clingers with their long and short legs. They can scamper right up the mountainside, short legs on the inside, long legs on the outside. If you want to sell that shaggy varmint to a zoo, I'll see what I can do."

"Thank you, no," replied Clarence sharply. So that's what the scheming red-tailed hawk had in mind. "Kindly be gone, sir."

"Yeah," said the show-off squirrel.

The hawk gave a little chuckle and flew off.

"So that's what I am," muttered the Windblown Child in wonder. "A Sidehill Clinger."

"You can't believe everything Thump Oswald says," remarked Clarence.

"We could build a steep hill and see if the Windblown Child can climb it," said the squirrel.

It took only a couple of days for the beavers and squirrels and skunks and possums and raccoons, working together around the clock, to throw up a small hill. It was shaped like an upside-down ice-cream cone.

And up the Sidehill Clinger went, clockwise, her short legs on the inside, her long legs on the outside. When she reached the top, she felt as triumphant as if she had climbed the highest mountain peak. From up there she could see clear over to Barefoot Mountain, sitting blue as chalk on the horizon.

"I reckon she's a Sidehill Clinger, all right," Clarence had to admit.

Watching her up there day after day, he recognized the sad look of homesickness in her eyes. He'd become accustomed to the sweet-tempered Windblown Child and would miss her; nevertheless, he went over to the beaver. "Can you make a couple of peg legs?"

"Most certainly," said the beaver.

He picked out a strong cottonwood branch and began to gnaw away. When the Windblown Child climbed down from the hill, the beaver was waiting with two peg legs. He took some measurements, chewed an inch or so off the ends, and smiled like a true craftsman. "Done," he announced proudly.

Clarence had brought some stout cord from his treasures and tied the pegs to the animal's short legs.

"Now let's see how you walk," said Clarence.

A burst of applause went up as the Windblown Child strutted as straight as a stilt-walker to the creek and back. The peg legs worked fine.

"I reckon you'll want to go home now," said Clarence.

"I reckon so," said the Sidehill Clinger.

But it was hard to leave her friends. She said her good-byes the following morning, and then went around on her peg legs and said good-bye all over again.

Clarence fixed up a picnic lunch. He didn't like the look of Thump Oswald circling overhead. The hawk's wings stretched out like claws in the sky. His tail looked dipped in blood.

So Clarence awakened the skunk, who had been up all night, and they joined the Sidehill Clinger peg-legging it to Barefoot Mountain.

They stopped for a picnic, and the skunk gave a yawn and fell asleep. Before long they were underway again. Soon the red-tailed hawk was circling overhead. Clarence began to feel nervous.

"Let's hurry," he said.

Now they were close enough to smell the pine trees on Barefoot Mountain, and the skunk began to doze off and walk in his sleep.

And that's when a dented pick-up truck with a big cage in it came roaring around the cactus and through the brush.

Two men in sweaty hats jumped out. They carried ropes and began spinning loops in the air.

"That thingamabob won't be hard to catch," one of them shouted. "You go around and rope it from behind."

Clarence shook the skunk furiously. "Wake up! What are you waiting for? Do what skunks do!"

But even before the skunk could get his target fixed and turn his back and lift his tail to attack, the ropes came flying through the air. They made ringers around the Sidehill Clinger's neck.

It was only when the men tightened up on the ropes that Clarence saw a change in the Windblown Child's sweet and peaceful disposition. Temper flashed up as red as fire in her eyes.

The forward peg leg swung out in a blue streak and knocked the front man rolling like a tumblebug. The Sidehill Clinger kicked his hind peg leg and the second man went flying so high he knocked Thump Oswald out of the sky. Both fell to earth in a shower of hawk's feathers.

"Bravo!" Clarence shouted. "I believe there is a touch of the spotted leopard in you after all!"

And then the skunk gave the villains a shower of skunk mist for good measure.

At the foot of the mountain Clarence untied the peg legs. The Windblown Child gave him an embrace. The pack rat dropped a tear. Then the Sidehill Clinger scampered up the steep and narrow trail, her short legs on the inside, her long legs on the outside.

"Be sure to save these peg legs and come visit us flatlanders!"

"I aim to, dear Clarence," replied the Sidehill Clinger before vanishing among the pine trees of Barefoot Mountain.

Yellercat

Yellercat, who lived with Mrs. Pickle in the shadow of Barefoot Mountain, was afraid to go outside. She loved to lie in the shade of the cottonwood tree in the front yard. But how could she nap and purr when Mad Dog had moved in across the road?

"Go outside and play," Mrs. Pickle would say, holding open the screen door. "You need fresh air and sunshine."

So Yellercat would stick her head out and gaze across the road. Only when Mad Dog was nowhere in sight would she lift her tail and venture out.

Life had been so peaceful before a pipsqueak tornado had shaken some carnival trucks like dice on the Barefoot

Mountain road. When the carnival had righted itself and continued on its way, Mad Dog had got left behind. Old Mr. Scrumple, meaning well, had found the cur and taken it in.

On Tuesday Yellercat ventured out. She had hardly finished sharpening her claws on the cottonwood tree when the carnival dog came loping over the spiked fence.

Off Yellercat streaked around back, through the cactus garden, and toward the kitchen. Off Mad Dog streaked after her.

Yellercat banged through the cat door. In came Mad Dog, snapping his teeth behind her. Only his broad shoulders stopped him. There he stood with his head framed inside the cat door, like a stuffed beast come to life. His crooked fangs dripped and clacked.

"Ruffian!" shouted Mrs. Pickle. "Bully! Coward, chasing a little thing of a cat!"

When Mad Dog saw her pick up a spray bottle to give him a squirt of water, he ducked his head out of range and

trotted home. Yellercat, now watching through the window, saw him cross the road, chest out, as if he owned the town, population 387.

Oh, I wish someone from the carnival would claim him and take him away, thought Yellercat. But no one did.

On a late afternoon Yellercat noticed the red-headed kids next door dressing up for Halloween. Kevin was blowing up a balloon with a snarly monster's face on it. Every time Kevin blew, the monster got bigger. And bigger. Out came its great white fangs and its bloodshot eyes.

And Yellercat saw that for once Mad Dog was tied up. So outside she went, tail high, and decided to follow the kids as they went trick-or-treating.

She'd hardly reached the crossroads when she heard a snarl and a growl and a *bark, bark, bark.* She turned, and there came Mad Dog. The rope flying from his collar snapped the air like a bullwhip. He'd broken loose and was racing right for her.

Yellercat wanted to run, but her legs froze to the path. Suddenly remembering Kevin and the monster balloon, she took a breath and blew herself up. She gulped down another breath, then blew herself up some more. With her fur standing out stiff as a wire, she swallowed a huge breath until she thought she'd burst her skin.

She felt as big and fierce as a bobcat. A lion, even!

His jaws wide open and his rusty teeth slathering, Mad Dog was almost upon her. Facing him, Yellercat put a huge arch in her back and spit. She spit like a burst of forked lightning. It was loud enough to break the post office window.

Mad Dog skinned his front paws putting on the brakes. He was dumbfounded. What happened to that shy and puny cat? Where had this lion come from?

With a yelp Mad Dog turned around to beat it. He knocked over the postmistress, who bit him on the leg.

And Yellercat walked home, chest out, her tail hoisted high as a kite. She walked past Mad Dog's house as if she owned the road.

Mad Dog had nightmares after that, and hid under the house whenever he saw Yellercat pass.

Emperor Floyd

After the tornado left, Floyd, the scruffy red rooster, developed insomnia. Whereas he used to crow just before dawn, now he was apt to wake up at two or three or four in the morning and disturb the neighbors.

"Hey, pipe down, rooster-bird!" cried the show-off squirrel.

"Stop your crowin'!" shouted a beaver.

"Shut your face!" croaked a bullfrog from the nearby creek.

Floyd gave his wings a stretch and crowed again. He had a mean streak in him. If he couldn't sleep, no one was going to sleep.

The next morning, hardly past two or three, Floyd again raised his voice to the sky. *"Cock-a-doodle-doooooooooo!"*

"Hey, Floyd, bag your head!"

"Shush up!"

"Rooster-bird, give your tonsils a rest!"

But Floyd crowed on with delight. He felt like an emperor in command of the peasantry. With an aloof gaze he'd watch as the possums and other night animals, thinking it must be almost daybreak, returned to their hollow trees and nests. They'd twiddle their thumbs until dawn.

Soon the rooster began thinking of himself as Emperor Floyd. And he was eating like royalty as well. A daytime rooster, going to bed as the sun went down, he rarely saw a firefly. But now, arising when he did, he saw a banquet of fireflies in the pitch-dark air.

He loved fireflies! Blinking, delectable morsels! He feasted!

And he grew fat on fireflies. His voice became bigger and carried further. It wouldn't surprise him if folks could hear Emperor Floyd all the way in the village.

"Cock-a-doodle-dooooooooooo!" he crowed with the silken notes of an opera singer.

The show-off squirrel, who had been pleasantly snoring, jumped out of his nest and pitched a hickory nut at Emperor Floyd. It was then the rooster noticed that there was something distinctly wrong with the squirrel's shadow.

"Have you been sick?" asked Emperor Floyd. "Some rare disease, no doubt. My good fellow, you're casting a shadow in the dark."

"Of course I am, you nitwit rooster-bird," said the squirrel. "That's because I'm standing in the light. You've gorged on so many lightning bugs that you glow in the dark."

"Nonsense," said Emperor Floyd. Surely, he thought, they must be standing in a shaft of moonshine.

"See for yourself," said the squirrel.

When they walked to the edge of the creek, Emperor Floyd saw his ghostly reflection in the water. His wings gave an involuntary flutter. Horrors! It was true! He glowed! He was bright as a full moon!

"Better make out your will," advised the show-off squirrel. "Coyotes will be able to see you a mile off. I hear one in the distance now."

Emperor Floyd began to tremble. He could hear the coyote, too. Running for high weeds, he tried to hide himself. But he could see the weeds light up around him as if he were a bonfire.

"Yip, yip, ahh-oohooohooo!"

He could hear the coyote advancing toward him. Emperor Floyd spied a hollow log and ran, but he never reached the hiding place. In his panic he ran right through the legs of a farmer, Deaf Bob, on the road.

Deaf Bob snatched up the rooster and gave a surprised little chuckle. "Well, look at you. Come along home with me."

Emperor Floyd felt a gasp of relief to be so suddenly saved from the coyote.

When the animals saw him carried off by Deaf Bob, the beaver said, "Now we can get some sleep around here. That rooster's heading for the cooking pot."

"Not Floyd," said the show-off squirrel. "That old rooster-bird's too tough to eat."

And the squirrel was right. Deaf Bob didn't cook up the rooster. He put the bird in a cage. He found a big rusty hook and hung Emperor Floyd in front of his house as a porch light.

Stumblefrog

There were many young bullfrogs like Webster who were growing up along the perky little creek east of Barefoot Mountain.

They tried out their voices at night, croaking as best they could. During the day they learned to leap and jump and kick their legs.

But not Webster. He was so clumsy he'd stumble over a dried-up crack in the earth. When he tried to jump, he'd trip on his own feet and skin his nose.

"There goes Stumblefrog," his friends began to shout. After that no one called him Webster anymore except for his mother.

"Webster, my sweet," said his mother, "go out and play with the other frogs."

Webster could see the other frogs in the cottonwood shade of the creek, jumping for the sheer joy of springing their legs. Now they were jumping to see who could make the longest leap.

"I don't want to play," said Webster, turning away.

When no one was looking, Webster would try to spring his legs into a froggy leap. But over he'd go, skinning his nose again. And almost always one of the animals would catch sight of him and shout, "Hey, look. There's Stumblefrog stumbling again! He just tripped over his own shadow!"

Not long after, Webster kissed his mother good-bye and left the creek. No longer would he have to listen to the taunts and yapping of the other frogs. No longer would the name Stumblefrog ring out in the cottonwoods.

He followed the creek for a while, feeding on black gnats and mosquitoes. Then he decided to cross the road. There, snagged on some green cactus, he saw a tornado-ripped canvas sign of a carnival fire-eater with flaming torches in his hands.

And that's where Webster found the carnival sack of dried beans, ripped wide open. The beans had not only spilled out in the dirt, they seemed on the move all around, like tumblebugs.

Astonishing! thought Webster, who had never before seen Mexican jumping beans. They twitched and shook themselves and rolled over and hopped about.

"Look at that one!" Webster shouted. "It jumped like a flea!"

He watched it a while longer. And then a sudden idea came crashing into his head. "What if . . . ?" he asked himself. "What if . . . ? What if . . . !"

He swallowed a bean. He swallowed another. They were awfully dry to swallow, and not nearly as tasty as mosquitoes and spiders. He ate so many Mexican jumping beans that his stomach grew huge and as lumpy as a bunch of grapes.

Hardly a moment passed before the beans began to work. There came a churning in his stomach as if a big hiccup was about to explode.

"A hiccup?" he muttered, greatly disappointed. "Is that all you flea-jumping beans can do? A hiccup?"

But suddenly the hiccup shot downward into Webster's legs. He felt his muscles tighten into springs. An instant later—*kachunk kabang!*—Webster felt himself shot high into the air. He knocked a tail feather off a red-tailed hawk passing overhead.

"Excuse me, sir," Webster cried out in mid-air.

"Watch where you're jumping!" exclaimed the hawk, who smelled strongly of skunk.

A huge smile swept across Webster's face. He was *jumping*! Jumping at last!

"Wait till the other frogs see me!"

The muscles in his legs coiled again, and once more he leaped into the air. How wonderful it felt!

How grand!

Like a bouncing ball he hurried back to the creek, where the other young frogs were finishing a jumping contest.

"Wait for me!" yelled Webster.

In he bounced, and—*kachunk kabang!*—off he shot into the air.

"Is that Stumblefrog?" the show-off squirrel cried out as Webster sailed over the heads of the frogs and won the contest.

"You may call me Webster!" said Webster.

He returned to the roadside jumping beans a couple of times, but only for the amusement of watching them tumble about like little acrobats. He quickly discovered that his legs had caught on to the trick of jumping. He could leap into the air fast and any time he wished. He had legs of steel.

"Webster," said the show-off squirrel one day, "if you jump any faster, you'll jump right out of your skin."

The Pitchfork Giant

J. J. Jones, a 400-pound backwoods hog, was no prize-winner. His hide was so muddy that weeds sprouted on his back. His ears were so dirty that potatoes really did grow out of them. Not only that, he was a thief.

"Did you steal the hickory nuts I had stored under that broken-down porch?" asked the show-off squirrel, pointing off toward the abandoned farmhouse.

"Of course not, my dear fellow," answered J. J., who was especially polite and well mannered when he was lying. "It must have been Lonesome John himself. You know how gone-minded that farmer was."

The animals had run wild ever since Lonesome John had wandered away after the noisy little tornado had touched down. He'd never come back. So everyone had to fend for himself.

J. J. Jones had taken possession of a patch of cottonwoods. It had a nice mud hole in it and a certain amount of dark and gloomy privacy. Dried poison ivy hung as thick as burlap curtains from the trees. It was there that he stored the things he stole and the things he didn't.

One day he was rooting around in the farmyard when he turned up a big brass harmonica. He recalled Lonesome John playing that thing on summer nights with the sun setting behind Barefoot Mountain. He remembered how the music had surged through his young veins like sap rising in a tree. The music had come out of his hooves, so that he kicked, stomped, and toe-danced to beat all.

J. J. Jones washed out the harmonica in the creek and blew on it and taught himself to play "Turkey in the Straw." By trial and error he found every note but two or three.

"Who taught you to play that thing?" asked the possum, who remembered the old days.

"I taught myself," said J. J. Jones. "Nothing smarter than a hog. Didn't Lonesome John used to say so?"

"Let's hear it again," said a bullfrog. "It sure beats cat-on-the-fence yowling."

After playing it once more, the 400-pound hog started home. But the animals followed him like a parade following a band.

"Let me tootle on that thing," asked the raccoon.

"Me, too," said the possum.

"No, gentlemen. No one touches this mouth organ but me. Keep your mitts off."

For days J. J. Jones played the harmonica for his own delight, crossing his legs and beating time. The sky seemed bluer. The stolen corn tasted juicier, and the mud in the swamp felt more soothing.

But being a thief himself, J. J. Jones assumed that everyone was a thief. He began to worry that one of the

other animals would steal the brass harmonica. He woke
up in a sweat and buried the harmonica under a mossy rock
and then under a board and then under an old, worn-out
horseshoe.

But what if someone had seen him?

The next morning, when a pack rat turned up and began
to nose around, J. J. Jones said, "I wouldn't go in them
woods, Clarence."

"Why not?"

"There's something in there, and it don't look friendly.
It's a giant."

"No giants live around here," said the pack rat.

"This one just moved in. I saw it. Big enough to squash you with its great toe. The creature picks his teeth with a pitchfork."

"I declare," said Clarence, and scurried away.

Not long after, when a porcupine came along, J. J. Jones called out, "Stop in your tracks, neighbor! The giant in the timber'll get you."

"I don't see any giant tracks."

"You will, the moment before he gobbles you up, quills and all. He shoots smoke and fire out of his nose. Has great bulging eyes, too. Big as pumpkins. Teeth like a rusty iron fence. He sits and picks his teeth with a pitchfork. I've seen him do it."

"A pitchfork? My, oh my," said the porcupine, and decided against venturing into the woods.

News of the Pitchfork Giant got around, and J. J. Jones added details as they occurred to him. The creature could turn himself invisible and pounce on you like a flash of lightning. The hair on his arms was sharp as cactus thorns.

Now J. J. Jones could slumber comfortably, certain that no one would go snooping into the woods and make off with the brass harmonica. It lay safely buried for months.

A gloomy fall day came along when J. J. Jones felt the sap rising in his soul. A little music in the air would make the sky seem blue again and the mud hole more pleasant.

"I think I'll get Lonesome John's mouth organ," he told himself.

Looking around to make sure he wasn't seen, he headed deeper into the woods. He brushed aside long drifts of poison ivy. At the same time a blind mole coming out of his burrow banged into the old, worn-out horseshoe. *Clang!*

"What was that!" shouted J. J. Jones, in a sudden lather of fear. "A pitchfork?"

"Ouch!" the mole cried out.

"What? What?" J. J. Jones's heart was jumping like a toad

inside his chest. "Is that you, Giant? Is that you picking your teeth with a pitchfork?"

Hiding behind a tree, J. J. Jones gulped for air and peered around. He saw nothing but dried poison ivy blowing in the breeze.

"Maybe you turned yourself invisible!" exclaimed the hog nervously. And he recalled that with one blast of fire from the monster's nose J. J. Jones would sizzle like bacon.

He was too terrified to move for several breaths. Finally, with his heart now clattering like an old windmill, J. J. Jones shot out of the cottonwoods.

He stood for a moment, shaking all over. "I saw him!" he began to shout. "The Pitchfork Giant. In there! Behind those trees. I saw him with my own eyes! Out of my way!"

J. J. Jones fled from the cottonwoods and never looked back.

And he never came back, either.

Without a few notes of music, J. J. Jones had nothing to kick his feet to on a gloomy day. The sky never again seemed as blue, or mud as wonderfully muddy.

A crow brought back news, a year or so later, that J. J. Jones was over in the next county. "He has punied up so skinny that his ribs stick out like a washboard," said the crow. "And a dozen vultures follow him wherever he goes."

As for the harmonica, the mole butted it out of his way. With a glint of brass, up it flew into the air. It landed in the crotch of a tree and stuck there tight.

Now, when the wind is blowing, a note or two of a mouth organ can be heard. When the wind is blowing just right, the cottonwood animals can hear whole chords softly drifting through the trees.

And the sky seems bluer. The neighbors seem more lighthearted. And the view of Barefoot Mountain seems more joyous.

Good-bye, Barefoot Mountain

Going jiggety joggedy over Barefoot Mountain, the no-account little tornado never came back. But there was still some mischief left in it.

Down the road from the cottonwoods it picked up a bald-headed farmer named Gunnysack Smith. Gunnysack got tumbled around as if he'd been sucked up into a cement mixer. He went flying about, bald head over bare heels.

When the tornado pitched him back on the road, Gunnysack Smith discovered that he had a full head of hair.

It wasn't hair, exactly. It was the long, spotted wool of a young Sidehill Clinger.

THE END